AUG - - 2015

THe FLYING HaND of MaRCo B.

Written by Richard Leiter & Illustrated by Shahar Kober

The seat belts fasten with a **CLICK**.
The door lock snaps shut with a **SNICK**.
The engine chugs on with a **CHURRRRR**.
The window comes down with a **WHURRRR**.

Now I'm rolling down the street.
The wind is blowing strong and sweet.
And only I can truly see
The Flying Hand of Marco B.

The Flying Hand that swoops and soars
　　　Beyond the windows, out the doors.
I put it up there in the sky
　　　'Cause only I can make it fly.

　　　My fingers float without a care
　　　　　　But as I'm swooping through the air
　　　My mommy's voice yells from afar,

But up the door my fingers crawl
And out the window go them all.
And once again I'm thrilled to see
The Flying Hand of Marco B.!

The wind is blowing all around!
The Flying Hand zooms up and down!
And as I reach the perfect glide...

Why can't the grown-ups understand?
I can't control this crazy hand.
Again it drifts outside the car...
Oh no! This time it's gone too far!

The seat belt cannot keep me in.
I'm being **SUCKED OUT** by the wind!
And like a little shooting star
I'm **FLYING** right above our car.

I twist my hands to fly around
A little up, a little down.
Below I see our car drives on...
Why, they don't even know I'm gone!

Right-side up and upside down
  I loop-the-loop above my town.
And way below, beside the mall
  I see my house—it looks so small.

Then up and up through flocks of seagulls
'Til I'm looking **DOWN** on eagles.
I flip my hands and yell out loud,
Then all at once ...

... I'm in a cloud.

The earth's so big, so blue, so vast.
How'd I get so high... so fast?
It's scary this far off the ground.
How'm I gonna get back down?

But even though I twist around,
I'm flying **UP** instead of down.
Going up was quick and breezy—
Going down?... It ain't so eeeeeeasy.

Now the **MOOOOON** begins to glisten.
Marco B., you just don't listen!
Where's my family to calm me?
Now I'm scared! I want my **MOMMMYYYYY!**

If only I could make this end
I'd **NEVER** fly the hand again.
I curl into a little ball
And just like that ...

... I start to fall.

One arm straight, one by my side,
Move my hands and I can glide.
Zooming down, I'm taking aim
And flying back the way I came.

Clouds and planes—I'm soaring down;
Seagulls, eagles—there's my town!
The mall, my house, and not too far
I see the road . . . and there's our car!

Now above the car I roll,
    Through the window, that's my goal.
Crawl into the car seat fast,
    Click the seat belt, safe at last!

There's my sister, Mom, and Dad.
No one noticed! No one's mad!
They're listening to the radio.
I'm back, I'm home . . . they'll never know.

I promise that on every ride
I'll always keep my hand inside.
But now I've told myself a lie—
The truth is this: **I LOVE to FLY!**

And once again I'll set it free...

THE FLYING HAND OF MARCO B.!

This book is dedicated to Rick,
a personal friend of Marco B.

–Richard

Sleeping Bear Press
315 E. Eisenhower Parkway, Suite 200
Ann Arbor, MI 48108
www.sleepingbearpress.com

Printed and bound in the United States.

10 9 8 7 6 5 4 3 2 1

Library of Congress Cataloging-in-Publication Data

Leiter, Richard.
The flying hand of Marco B. / written by Richard Leiter ;
illustrated by Shahar Kober.
pages cm
Summary: "Marco is riding in the backseat of a car driven by his parents.
Being bored, he puts his hand out the window and fantasizes about flying. As he does so,
his fantasy takes him on a wild ride up in the sky"– Provided by the publisher.
ISBN 978-1-58536-888-4
[1. Stories in rhyme. 2. Flight–Fiction. 3. Imagination–Fiction.
4. Automobile driving–Fiction.] I. Kober, Shahar, illustrator. II. Title.
PZ8.3.L5346Fl 2014
[E]–dc23
2013027384